Earaches

Dr. Alvin Silverstein,

Virginia Silverstein, and

Laura Silverstein Nunn

My Health

Franklin Watts

A Division of Scholastic Inc.

New York • Toronto • London • Auckland • Sydney

Mexico City • New Delhi • Hong Kong

Danbury, Connecticut

Photographs © 2001: Corbis-Bettmann: 10 (Lester V. Bergman), 11 left (Kevin Fleming); Custom Medical Stock Photo: 26 (Logical Images), 30 (Jon Meyer), 9, 23 (NMSB); Nance S. Trueworthy: 32; Peter Arnold Inc./Laura Dwight: 11 right; Photo Researchers, NY: 19 (Biophoto Associates/SS), 16 (A.B. Dowsett/SPL), 6, 28 (Blair Seitz), 4 (John Watney/SS); PhotoEdit: 38 (David K. Crow), 13 (Myrleen Ferguson), 24 (Tony Freeman), 14, 33 (Spencer Grant), 35 (Michael Newman), 29 (D. Young-Wolff); Rigoberto Quinteros: 21, 27, 36; Visuals Unlimited: 7 bottom (Rick & Nora Bowers), 18 (David M. Phillips), 7 top (D. Yeske).

Cartoons by Rick Stromoski

Library of Congress Cataloging-in-Publication Data

Silverstein, Alvin.
    Earaches / by Alvin Silverstein, Virginia Silverstein, and Laura Silverstein Nunn.
        p. cm.—(My Health)
    Includes bibliographical references and index.
    ISBN 0-531-11873-8 (lib. bdg.)   0-531-15562-5 (pbk.)
    1. Earache in children—Juvenile literature. 2. Earache—Juvenile literature
[1. Earache. 2. Ear—Diseases. 3. Diseases. 4. Hearing. 5. Senses and sensation.]
I. Silverstein, Virginia B. II. Nunn, Laura Silverstein III. Title IV. Series
RF291.5.C45 S55   2002
618.92'0978–dc21   2001017569

Contents

My Ear Hurts!

You were fighting a bad cold all week. You felt hot and tired, your head hurt, and you couldn't stop sneezing—you felt just plain awful. Your nose got really sore, too, from blowing it so much. Now, just when you're finally getting over your cold, your ear starts to hurt. What's happening? You have an earache. You need to see a doctor.

Most earaches occur after a cold or allergy develops. When you have a cold, for instance, your nose produces a lot of fluid. Sometimes fluid builds up in the ear and provides a home for germs. This may lead to an ear **infection**.

Did You Know...

Earaches are the second most common illness in children, next to common colds.

◀ This boy is suffering from a cold. Most earaches occur after a cold develops.

You can also get an earache by sticking something such as your finger, into your ear. The skin inside your ear is very thin and can be damaged easily. So putting anything into your ear can cause it to itch and hurt.

Earaches should be checked out by a doctor. Most of the time, earaches can be treated easily with medicine. But in some rare cases, an ear infection can lead to permanent hearing loss.

Read on and learn more about your amazing ears, how ear problems develop, and what you can do to you protect yourself from getting earaches in the first place.

This girl's doctor is checking to see if she has an ear infection.

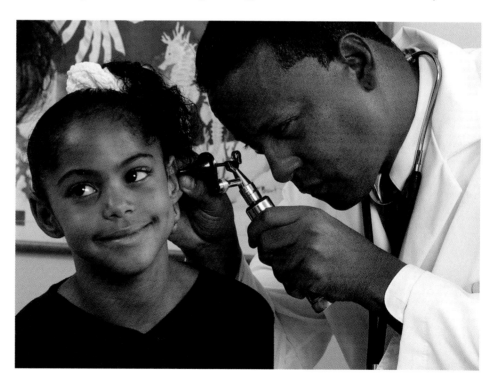

Inside the Ear

When you look at yourself in the mirror, you can see only part of your ears. Even somebody looking at you from the side does not see your whole ear. The most important parts of your ears are hidden inside your head.

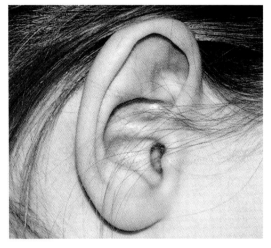

Your ear is made up of three main parts: the outer ear, the middle ear, and the inner ear. The only part that you can see is the **pinna**, a part of the outer ear. The pinna has a large earflap and a narrow opening, which helps to channel sounds into the inner parts of the ear.

The only part of the ear you can see is called the pinna.

Listen Up!

Animals with large pinnae, such as elephants, foxes, and rabbits, can hear better than you can. That's partly because their large ears channel sounds directly into the ear, just as a funnel helps to channel liquids into the neck of a narrow bottle.

The antelope jackrabbit can hear well because of its large ears.

7

Activity 1:
Sound Funnels

Have a friend speak to you very softly from across the room. Now cup your hand behind your ear, moving your pinna forward. Can you hear your friend more clearly? What about background noises, like an air conditioner or fan? Do they sound different, or louder? You can make an even more effective "hearing aid." Cut out a triangle with two equal sides that are at least 10 inches long from a large piece of cardboard. Cut off about an inch from the angle between the two equal sides, then curl the cardboard into a cone and tape the two edges together. Hold the cone with the small end over your ear canal and turn your head so that your ear is pointing toward a sound, such as your friend talking. Try listening with and without the cardboard sound funnel.

Sound travels through the air in invisible waves called **sound waves**. Sounds that are collected in the pinna travel through a tube called the **ear canal**. The skin that lines the ear canal contains special glands that produce sticky, yellowish **earwax**. You may think that earwax is yucky stuff, but it is actually very helpful. Earwax helps to keep the ear canal smooth and moist. It also traps insects, dust, and dirt so they don't go farther into the ear.

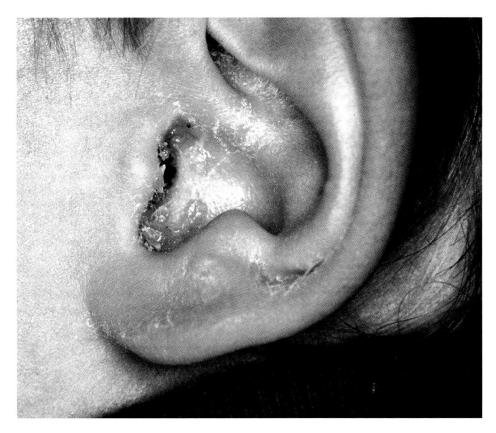

Earwax is helpful in keeping the ear canal smooth and moist, but this boy has too much earwax. He needs to clean his ears.

At the end of the ear canal, the sound waves hit a thin sheet of tissue called the **eardrum**. The eardrum is so sensitive that even the slightest sounds will make it **vibrate** (move back and forth). As the eardrum vibrates, it sends sound waves into the middle ear. The middle ear contains three tiny bones loosely attached together in a row—the hammer, the anvil, and the stirrup. They are named after the objects they are shaped like. The hammer rests on the eardrum. When the eardrum vibrates, its movements make the hammer start to jiggle. The jiggling hammer then strikes the anvil, causing it to vibrate too. The anvil, in turn, sends the vibrations into the stirrup, which rests on a thin sheet of tissue stretched across the "window" into the inner ear.

The eardrum vibrates when sound waves enter the ear.

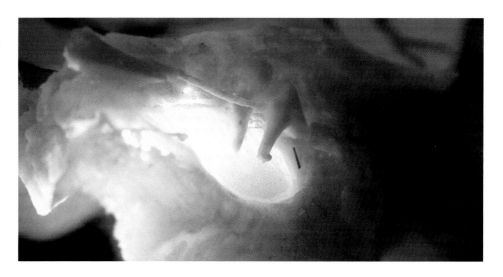

The middle ear contains an opening into a very important structure called the **eustachian** (yew-STAY-kee-an) **tube**. This is a narrow tube that connects the middle ear to the back of the nose and throat. The middle ear is filled with air, which is normally at the same pressure as the air outside. Most of the time the eustachian tube is closed, but it opens automatically whenever you swallow, yawn, or move your jaw in chewing. This allows air to pass between the throat and middle ear, which helps to keep the air pressure inside your ear equal to the air pressure outside your ear.

Small Bones

The bones in your ear—the hammer, the anvil, and the stirrup—are the smallest bones in your body.

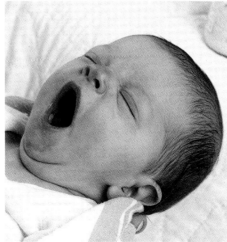

Yawning keeps the air pressure inside the ear the same as the air pressure outside the ear.

Ear Popping

Have your ears ever "popped" when you went up or down very quickly in an elevator or in an airplane? Why did this happen?

Normally, the eustachian tubes work well, keeping the air pressure inside your ears the same as the air pressure outside your ears. But when you ride in an elevator or take off in an airplane, the pressure outside changes too quickly for the middle ear to keep up, and the eustachian tubes may be squeezed shut. As a result, your ears may pop or squeak painfully, and you may have trouble hearing sounds clearly for a short time. Eventually, the air pressure in the middle ear will get back to normal and you will hear well again.

You can avoid this unpleasant feeling by swallowing or yawning, which helps to open the eustachian tubes. On an airplane, it's usually a good idea to chew gum during a takeoff or landing.

As sound vibrations enter your inner ear, they travel into the **cochlea** (COE-klee-uh), a tiny, fluid-filled, spiral tube that looks like a snail shell. The cochlea is lined with thousands of tiny hair cells, that move when sound waves hit them. A tiny, threadlike nerve fiber connects to each hair cell. The thousands of tiny nerve fibers from the hair cells are gathered into a rope of fibers called the **auditory nerve**, which is connected to the brain. As the hair cells move, messages are sent along the auditory nerve and are then carried to the brain. Special areas of the brain are devoted to receiving and analyzing messages sent from the ears. The brain makes sense out of the information it receives from the ears and turns it into something we can understand. This whole process makes it possible for you to listen to and understand the many sounds you hear every day, such as a ringing telephone, songs on the radio, or your friends' voices.

If anything goes wrong with any part of the ear, from the ear canal all the way into the cochlea, you may have trouble hearing.

The information sent from your ears to your brain, makes it possible for you to have a conversation with your friends.

What Is an Ear Infection?

Ear infections usually develop in the middle ear. In fact, this problem is sometimes called **otitis media**, which means middle-ear infection. An ear infection occurs when fluid builds up in the middle ear and becomes a breeding ground for **bacteria** (germs).

You are most likely to get an ear infection after having a cold or an allergy attack, when your nose

When your body produces a large amount of mucus, the fluid can build up inside your ear.

produces large amounts of fluid **(mucus)**. Normally, the fluid in the middle ear drains out into your throat through the eustachian tube. But sometimes when you're sick or having an allergic reaction, the eustachian tube gets swollen shut and fluid builds up in the middle ear. Then there is nowhere for the fluid to go. As fluid fills up the middle ear space, pressure builds up inside your ear and your ear starts to ache.

Why Do Kids Get So Many Ear Infections?

Ear infections are much more common in children than in adults. Kids younger than 3 years old get the most ear infections, but they are still common in kids up to age 8.

One reason why ear infections are so common in young kids is that their eustachian tubes are smaller than they are in older kids and in adults, and can get swollen shut more easily. Kids' eustachian tubes also don't slant downward as much as they do in adults, so fluids can't drain out as easily. As children grow older, the eustachian tubes get larger and turn downward at an angle.

Earache is the main symptom of an ear infection. Other signs of this condition may include stuffiness in the ear, fever, dizziness, loss of appetite, crankiness, and fluid draining from the ear.

The germs that cause colds are not the same germs that produce ear infections. Colds are caused by viruses,

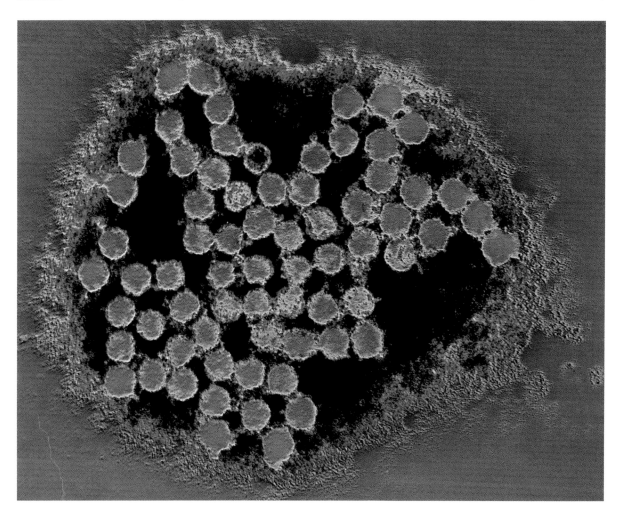

which are much tinier and simpler than bacteria. They get into the body when you breathe in tiny droplets of moisture that people with colds sneeze or cough out. Cold viruses may also sneak in if you touch something that somebody with a cold coughed on and then put your fingers to your nose, mouth, or eyes. In the warm, moist lining of the nose and throat, the viruses start to multiply.

The miserable, stuffed-up feeling you have when you have a cold is not really produced by the viruses. It is the result of the body's fight against them. Viruses multiply by taking control of body cells and turning them into little virus factories. Each cell makes huge numbers of new viruses. When the cells are finished producing them, the viruses burst out, killing the cells that made them. Then they spread out to infect other cells. When cells are injured by viruses, they send out chemicals that act as alarm signals. Some of these chemicals make fluid leak out of the blood vessels into the body tissues, making them swollen. The tissues then get hot and red-looking. This process is called **inflammation**.

Other chemicals produced by the damaged cells signal for help and call upon jellylike **white blood cells** that can travel through the blood and tissues.

This is what your white blood cells would look like if they were magnified more than 50,000 times.

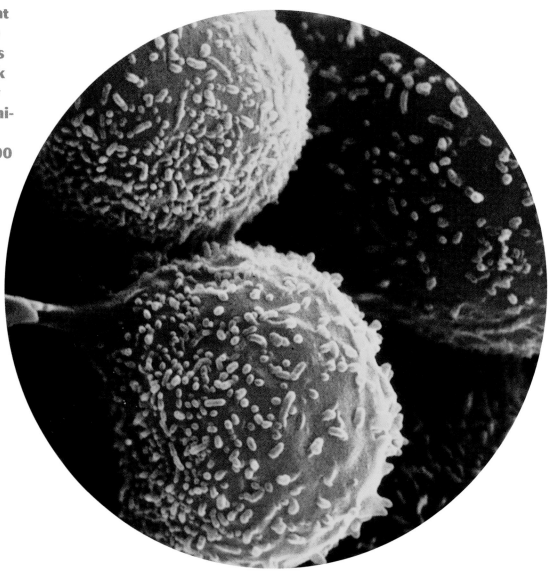

White blood cells can move most easily through inflamed, fluid-filled tissues. Some of them make chemical weapons that stop the viruses from multiplying, and others kill them directly. Others gobble up germs and damaged cells. But germs produce poisons, and after a white blood cell has eaten a lot of them, it dies. **Pus**, that yucky white stuff that builds up when you have an infection, is made up mainly of the bodies of dead white cells along with the germs they have killed.

Allergies can cause inflammation too. In people with allergies, the body's defenses react to harmless things such as pollen or dust, which don't bother most people at all. The body acts as though it were being

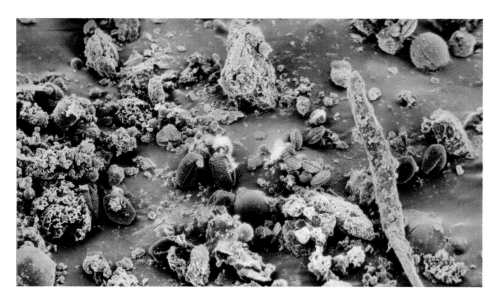

Pollen and dust particles can trigger allergies.

attacked by germs. Tissues get inflamed, and special white blood cells rush in.

No matter what causes it, inflammation of the nose and throat prepares the way for an ear infection. The germs that cause ear infections are bacteria that live in the throat. Some of them travel up through the eustachian tubes into the middle ear. Normally they don't cause trouble. But when the tissues lining the eustachian tubes swell, and fluid builds up in the middle ear, the bacteria are trapped inside. They start to multiply in their warm, cozy home. White blood cells move in to battle them. Soon the middle ear fills up with bacteria and pus. Pressure builds up, and the eardrum may bulge outward. This is painful. Sometimes the pressure is so great that the eardrum bursts and fluid and pus drain out. That's why some people have a white or yellowish fluid draining from the ear—it's the pus that built up during the infection. It looks different from earwax and it may have a bad smell.

Even if the eardrum does not burst, an ear infection can cause temporary hearing problems. Normally, the middle ear is filled with air, and the three tiny ear bones can vibrate readily whenever sounds hit the eardrums. But during an ear infection, when the middle ear is filled with fluid, the ear bones cannot vibrate as well. So, sounds seem muffled, and words may be harder to understand. If you press the palm of your hand tightly over one of your ears and listen to the television, you can hear the difference. It is hard to hear clearly with the ear that is covered.

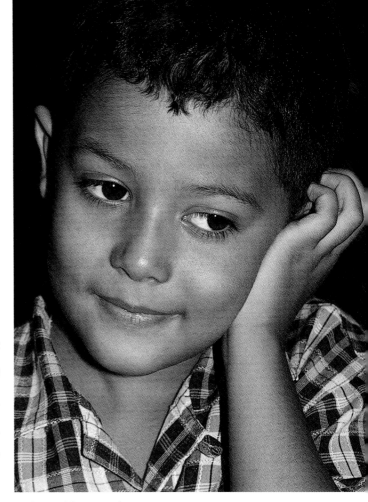

That's what your hearing might be like if you have an ear infection. In most cases your hearing recovers when the infection clears up. If the eardrum bursts, though, the hearing loss may be greater because the eardrum can't vibrate properly to send sounds into the ear.

Sometimes when you have an ear infection, you can only hear out of one ear.

Activity 2:
Sound Drums

For this activity you'll need three empty tin cans, some large, clean plastic bags, two wooden pencils, scissors, and tape. Cut out a circle from a plastic bag, that is two inches wider than the opening of one of the cans. Stretch it tightly over the open top of the can to make a drum and then tape around the edge to hold it in place. Do the same thing with the second can. Then, use the point of the scissors to punch a hole in the plastic cover after you have it taped onto the can. For the third drum, fill the can to the top with water before taping the plastic cover in place. (Don't make a hole in that one.) Now try tapping on each of the three drums, using the pencils as drum-sticks. Are there any differences in the sounds they make? Do you see why an eardrum cannot vibrate as well when the middle ear is filled with fluid? And what happens to the vibrations when there is a hole in the drum?

A burst eardrum is not really as bad as it sounds. Usually a tear in the eardrum heals up by itself within a week or so. But if the tear is very large, a doctor may have to repair it. If the ear infection is not caught early enough and treated properly, the damage could get worse, and hearing loss could be permanent.

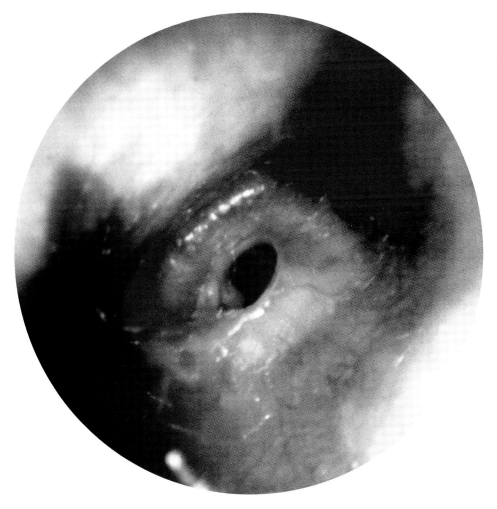

This eardrum has a large tear that needs to be repaired.

Swimmer's Ear

Have you ever gotten water in your ear when you went swimming? Your ear felt stuffed up and you couldn't hear sounds very clearly. You shook your head to try to empty the water out of your ear. Finally, the water came out and you could hear again.

Lots of people get water in their ears from time to time. Normally, the water runs out and the moisture dries up, and it doesn't cause any problems. But sometimes the wetness in your ear combined with the heat and humidity of summer can cause bacteria to grow in your ear canal. The bacteria produce an infection commonly known as **swimmer's ear**. Unlike a

Swimmer's ear got its name because it happens more often in the summer months, when people go swimming.

middle-ear infection, swimmer's ear is an infection of the *outer* ear: the ear canal just outside the eardrum.

Swimmer's ear may develop when the bacteria in your ear canal start to cause you trouble. Actually, you have bacteria living inside your ear canal all the time. Normally, they do not bother you. But if the conditions are just right—a nice, warm place with lots of moisture—the bacteria will grow and multiply. The earwax produced in the ear canal is supposed to protect the skin from infections. But when you go swimming or take a shower for a long period of time, you wash away much of the ear canal's protective wax coating. This makes it easier for bacteria to invade and cause an infection in your ear canal—swimmer's ear.

Swimmer's ear may also be caused by bacteria that live in lakes or reservoirs. When you take a swim in a lake, for instance, bacteria in the water enter your ears and can lead to an infection. Bacteria are not found in swimming pools and bath water because those water sources are usually treated with chemicals that kill them.

What does swimmer's ear feel like? When the ear canal becomes infected, your ear feels stuffed up and itchy. Scratching the itch, however, can cause more problems. You create openings in the skin, which allows bacteria to get inside. This can make the

What's a Boil?

Bacteria in the ear canal may also produce a **boil**, a hard, painful swelling just under the surface of the skin. Pus builds up and nearby tissues become hot and swollen. Some boils get better by themselves as the white blood cells win the battle and clear up the infection and the dead cells. But sometimes a boil just gets bigger and more painful. Then a doctor has to cut a small opening into the skin to let the boil drain.

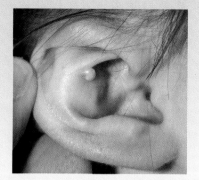

This child has a boil on her ear.

infection even worse, and your ear feels swollen and very painful when you touch it. This swelling closes the ear canal, making it very hard to hear out of the infected ear. You may also have a white or yellowish, bad-smelling fluid draining from the ear.

You can also get an infection in your ear canal when its skin lining is scratched or irritated, allowing bacteria to get in. This can happen when you stick something in your ear, such as a cotton swab. A buildup of earwax can also hurt the lining. Usually earwax dries up and falls out. But sometimes your ear makes too much earwax and it builds up. This may put pressure on the skin lining and irritate it. The earwax could also block your eardrum, causing temporary hearing loss.

Checking Out Earaches

Earache is a common symptom of a number of different conditions. It's not always easy to pinpoint exactly what is causing the pain in your ear. You should have an earache checked out by a doctor. The sooner, the

Test the Difference

Sometimes it's hard to tell the difference between a middle ear infection and swimmer's ear. You can do a little test that can help you figure out what's causing your earache. Pull your earlobe outward from your face. If it hurts a lot, you probably have swimmer's ear. Swimmer's ear often causes a lot of pain when you touch the earlobe or other outside parts of the ear. Pulling on your earlobe will not hurt if you have a middle ear infection.

This test is not always accurate, so you should still have a doctor take a look into your ear to make sure.

better—if the problem is serious and it is not treated early enough, it could lead to hearing loss.

A doctor will need to know all about your earache. When did you get it? How long have you had it? Have you had a cold recently? Do you have allergies? What other symptoms have you been having?

The doctor will then examine your ear with an **otoscope**, a special instrument that makes it easier to see inside your ear canal. An otoscope contains

The doctor uses an otoscope to examine your ears.

magnifying lenses that let the doctor get a close look at your eardrum. The doctor will first remove any earwax or particles that may be blocking the ear canal. If the ear canal appears red, flaky, and swollen, and there is a painful, pus-filled blister or boil, you probably have swimmer's ear.

You probably have an ear infection if the eardrum looks red and it bulges. The doctor may use a test called **tympanometry** in which

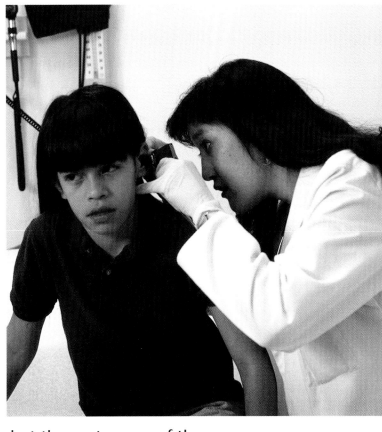

The doctor is checking to see if this girl has an ear infection.

a small, soft rubber tip is placed at the entrance of the ear canal. The equipment sends sound into the ear canal and measures how well the eardrum moves as the pressure changes. If the eardrum doesn't move as much as it should, then there's probably fluid in the middle ear. This test also shows if there's a hole in the eardrum, if the eustachian tube is draining correctly, and whether the little bones that transmit sound vibrations through the middle ear are working normally.

If the doctor thinks that the ear infection has affected your hearing, you may need to take a hearing test, which is given by a specialist called an **audiologist**. In this test, you wear headphones and listen to many different sounds. You let the audiologist know when you hear a sound. He or she will be able to tell if you have had any hearing loss.

Once the doctor has determined exactly what's wrong with your ear, he or she can decide on the best way to treat the problem.

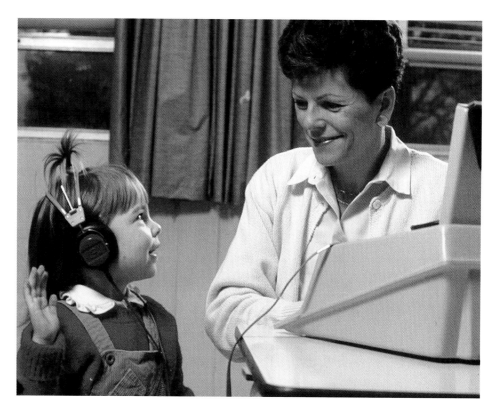

This child is having her hearing tested as part of her kindergarten screening.

Treating Earaches

Middle-ear infections are often treated with **antibiotics**, drugs that kill bacteria or stop them from growing. There are many different kinds of antibiotics. Some of them have to be taken for five days, while others are taken for ten to fourteen days. They can come in liquid or pill form. You may start to feel better after a couple of days. That's because the medicine is getting rid of the harmful bacteria.

Don't stop taking your medicine as soon as you are feeling good. The antibiotics haven't finished their job yet—they are still working hard to kill all the bacteria. Stopping the antibiotics too soon may allow the few strong bacteria that are left to multiply and cause your infection to return. These bacteria are **drug-resistant**—they can't be killed by the antibiotic. The doctor may have to give you a different drug to treat the infection.

Did You Know...

Some ear infections are caused by viruses. Antibiotics cannot kill viruses. Unfortunately, doctors cannot tell if an ear infection is caused by bacteria or viruses just by looking inside the ear.

Swimmer's ear is caused by different bacteria than the ones that cause middle-ear infections. So the two infections need to be treated differently. Oral antibiotics, which are taken through the mouth, do not work for swimmer's ear. Instead, swimmer's ear is treated with antibiotic eardrops. This medicine kills the bacteria that live on the skin in the ear canal and the ones under the skin, which are causing the inflammation.

It is very important to keep your ears dry when you have an ear infection. You should wear earplugs when you go swimming or when you bathe or shower.

Wearing earplugs can help keep water out of your ears when you swim.

Having an ear infection can make you feel miserable. While you're waiting for your medicine to work, you can do some things at home to make yourself feel better. Taking acetaminophen or ibuprofen will bring down the fever and ease the pain. Holding a warm compress against your ear can be soothing. Lying down may bother your ear. You may feel better if you prop your head up with pillows.

Most of the time, antibiotics clear up the ear infection. Sometimes, though, the symptoms seem to disappear, but the fluid remains in your ear. When the medicine is finished, the ear infection returns. Kids who cannot be helped by antibiotics, and get one ear infection after another, may need to have special tubes put in their eardrums. These are tiny tubes that are surgically placed through the eardrum into the middle ear so that fluid can drain properly. The tubes

Sleeping with your head propped up on pillows can sometimes help ease the pain of ear infections.

Turn Up the Volume

Do you say "huh?" or "what?" a lot when people talk to you? Do your parents complain that you play the stereo too loud? You might have a hearing problem.

A hearing aid might be what you need. This is a device that can allow you to "turn up the volume" and hear sounds better. It can be fitted into your outer ear. If you are afraid of how you'll look wearing a hearing aid, don't worry! It's cool to be able to hear what people are saying.

usually fall out by themselves within six to twelve months after they are put in. The tiny holes left by the tubes normally heal up without any problems. But sometimes the hole does not heal properly and a surgeon has to repair it. Some kids have to have ear tubes put in more than once if they continue to have ear infections. Eventually they outgrow the problem and no longer need the tubes.

It's very important to keep your ears dry if you have ear tubes. If water gets into the middle ear, it could be very painful and fluid may drain out. So wear earplugs when you go swimming or take a bath.

Ear infections that are not treated properly or early enough may lead to permanent hearing loss. Your eardrum or middle ear bones may be seriously damaged. Sounds may seem faint or muffled. You may have to turn up the radio or television. You might miss some words when people are talking to you. Hearing loss can also lead to difficulties in school because you may not hear everything your teacher says in class. The teacher may think that you have a learning problem when actually you have a hearing problem.

Fortunately, ear infections rarely lead to permanent hearing loss. But don't take any chances—if you have an earache, get it checked out so it can be treated right away.

This boy uses hearing aids to help him hear.

Preventing Earaches

There's an old saying, "Never put anything smaller than your elbow into your ear." That's some good advice. You shouldn't put anything like cotton swabs, paper clips, or even a finger into your ears to clean out earwax. You could scratch the ear canal and leave it open to infection. Sticking an object into your ear could also poke a hole in your eardrum. This could cause serious problems, such as hearing loss.

Sticking that pencil in her ear could lead to an infection or damage her eardrum.

If you want to clean your ears, use a washcloth and clean around the ear canal. Your self-cleaning earwax system should take care of itself. But if you have earwax buildup, especially if it's making it hard for you to hear, have a doctor remove it.

Since ear infections often develop after getting a cold, you should cut down your chances of catching one. To keep cold viruses from spreading to you, try not to touch people who have colds, wash your hands regularly, and always wash your hands before touching your eyes or nose.

Another important way you can keep from catching colds is staying healthy. You can do this by eating well, exercising regularly, getting enough rest, and practicing clean habits (washing your hands and keeping your body, clothes, food, and dishes clean). If you can keep yourself healthy and strong, then your body's defenses will be strong enough to fight off invading germs.

Did You Know...

When kids have had a lot of middle ear infections, doctors may give them antibiotics throughout the winter season when they are most likely to get sick. The drugs can fight off bacteria before they have a chance to multiply and cause an infection.

If you have allergies, you can also cut down your risk of ear infections by getting your allergies under control. Medicines can help to dry up your nose. You can also try to avoid the things that are causing your allergy. For instance, if you are allergic to dust, take the rugs out of your bedroom and try to keep your room as clean as possible. You can also use an air purifier, a device that removes dust particles from the air.

If you have an ear infection or an allergy, your doctor may prescribe a medication.

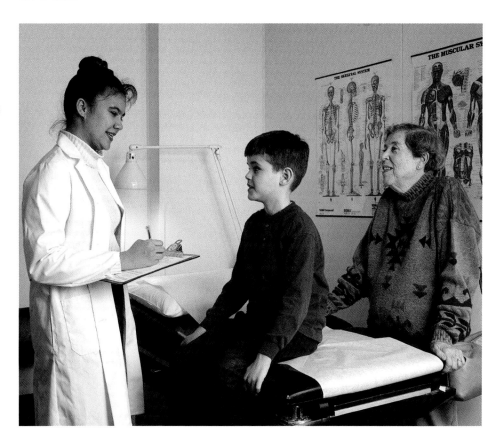

Don't Smoke by Me!

Some scientists believe that being around somebody who smokes may increase your chances of developing an ear infection. They say that cigarette smoke irritates the tissues in the middle ear and causes them to swell up. This makes it easier for viruses and bacteria to get in and cause an infection. In one study, they found that kids who lived with smokers were almost twice as likely to get middle-ear infections. They were also more likely to have allergies, which can also lead to swollen eustachian tubes and middle-ear infections.

Medical experts say that you can avoid getting swimmer's ear by putting a mixture of rubbing alcohol and vinegar in your ears after swimming. Your drugstore also sells an alcohol mixture for use after swimming. Your mom, dad, or some other grownup can put a few drops of this solution into your ears using an eardropper. The alcohol helps to dry the ear canal, and the vinegar works to keep bacteria from growing. You can also reduce your risk for swimmer's ear by wearing earplugs when you go swimming.

Take good care of your ears, and they'll be good for a lifetime of listening.

Glossary

antibiotic—a drug that kills bacteria or stops them from growing

audiologist—a specialist who tests hearing and helps to solve the problems involved with hearing loss

auditory nerve—a thick cord of nerve cells that sends signals from the ears to the brain, where they are translated into meaningful sounds

bacteria—germs; single-celled organisms too small to see without a microscope. Some bacteria cause diseases when they get into the body.

boil—a hard, painful, pus-filled swelling just under the surface of the skin caused by infection by bacteria

cochlea—fluid-filled, spiral-shaped tube in the inner ear that contains the organ for hearing. It looks like a snail shell.

drug-resistant germs—bacteria or viruses that are not killed by antibiotics

ear canal—a curved tube leading into the ear

eardrum—a thin, vibrating covering that stretches across the opening into the middle ear

earwax—a yellowish, sticky substance produced by special glands in the ear canal. It protects the ear canal from infection and traps insects, dirt, and dust.

eustachian tube—a tube that connects the middle ear to the back of the nose and throat

infection—invasion of the body by germs that multiply and damage tissues

inflammation—redness, heat, and swelling that develop when tissues are damaged

mucus—a gooey liquid produced by the cells in lining of the nose and breathing passages

otitis media—an infection of the middle ear

otoscope—a medical instrument used to examine the ear

pinna—the outer ear, including a large earflap and narrow opening (ear canal)

pus—a whitish substance containing the bodies of dead white blood cells and germs

sound waves—the form sound vibrations take as they travel through the air swimmer's ear—infection of the outer ear, or ear canal

tympanometry—a test used to measure how the eardrum moves. It also checks whether the eustachian tube is working properly, whether there's a hole in the eardrum, and whether sounds are being transmitted properly.

vibrate—to move back and forth

white blood cells—jellylike blood cells that can move through tissues and are an important part of the body's defenses. Some white blood cells eat germs and clean up bits of damaged cells and dirt.

Learning More

Books

Bluestone, Charles and Sylvan Stool. *Earache in Children: A Guide for Parents*, The Health Information Network, 1995.

Greene, Alan R. *The Parent's Complete Guide to Ear Infections*. New York: Avon Books, 1999.

Lansky, Vicki. *Koko Bear's Big Earache*. Minnetonka: Book Peddlers, 1990.

Online Sites

What is an Ear Infection?

http://kidshealth.org/kid/ill_injure/sick/ear_infection.html
This web site provides easy-to-understand information about ear infections.

Common Childhood Ear Problems

http://kidshealth.org/parent/general/eyes/summer_ear.html
This site provides information about swimmer's ear and ear problems that occur in airplanes.

Ear Infections and Children

http://www.medem.com/search/default.cfm
Type "ear infections" in the search box at this American Academy of Pediatrics site and click "Go" for links to ten articles about various aspects of ear infections.

Earaches

http://www.drreddy.com/earache.html

This site provides information on middle-ear infections and swimmer's ear. It also has links to fun sites for kids.

Ask the Scientist: Questions and Answers About Hearing

http://www.nidcd.nih.gov/health/kids/

This is a fun site with questions and answers about sound and hearing, classroom activities, and an interactive "sound ruler," provided by the National Institute on Deafness and Other Communication Disorders.

Children and Earwax

http://webmd.lycos.com/content/article/3172.10108

This site provides information about earwax and what you can do if you get earwax buildup.

Acute Otitis Media

http://www.nightimepediatrics.com/Parentedu/otitis.html

This is an article about ear infections by pediatrician Lynne Scannell, MD.

Another Ear Infection!?!

http://members.aol.com/fatdoc/otitis-m.htm

This is an article about the ear and middle ear problems by Warren P. Silberstein, MD.

Index

Page numbers in *italics* indicate illustrations.

About the Authors

Dr. Alvin Silverstein is a professor of biology at the College of Staten Island of the City University of New York. **Virginia B. Silverstein** is a translator of Russian scientific literature. The Silversteins first worked together on a research project at the University of Pennsylvania. Since then, they have produced 6 children and more than 170 published books for young people.

Laura Silverstein Nunn, a graduate of Kean College, has been helping with her parents' books since her high school days. She is the coauthor of more than fifty books on diseases and health, science concepts, endangered species, and pets. Laura lives with her husband Matt and their young son Cory in a rural New Jersey town not far from her childhood home.